Waiting

written by
Glenn Coats
illustrated by
Gloria Gedeon

KAEDEN ❦ BOOKS™

I am waiting by a hollow log.
I'm still and quiet waiting
for a frog.

2

I see a bird fly by me.

A mosquito buzzes in my ear.

I am waiting by a hollow log.
I'm still and quiet waiting
for a frog.

I see spiders on the water.

A dragonfly lands.

I am waiting by a hollow log.
I'm still and quiet waiting
for a frog.

I see a butterfly sit on a flower. A snake slithers through the leaves.

I am waiting by a hollow log.
I'm still and quiet waiting
for a frog.

I see ants crawling on the log.
A rabbit hops past me.

I was waiting by a hollow log.
I was still and quiet, but no frog.